W9-AWV-619

MUSIC in the WOOD

With love to
our wonderful
granddaughter
Meghan
on her tenth birthday!

From Grampop
and grandma Holly—

MUSIC
in the

BY CORNELIA CORNELISSEN

PHOTOGRAPHED BY JOHN MacLACHLAN

WOOD

DELACORTE PRESS

Special thanks to Marten Cornelissen, Roel Dieltiens, and Christine Pratt

Published by
Delacorte Press
Bantam Doubleday Dell Publishing Group, Inc.
1540 Broadway
New York, New York 10036

Text copyright © 1995 by Cornelia Cornelissen
Photographs copyright © 1995 by John MacLachlan

All rights reserved. No part of this book may be reproduced or transmitted in any form
or by any means, electronic or mechanical, including photocopying, recording, or by any
information storage and retrieval system, without the written permission of the Publisher,
except where permitted by law.

The trademark Delacorte Press® is registered in the U.S. Patent and Trademark Office.

Library of Congress Cataloging-in-Publication Data

Cornelissen, Cornelia.
     Music in the wood / by Cornelia Cornelissen ; photographed by John MacLachlan.
          p.   cm.
     ISBN 0-385-31167-2
          1. Violoncello—Construction—Juvenile literature.
     I. MacLachlan, John. ill. II. Title.
ML911.C67 1995
787.4' 1923—dc20   94-33470 CIP AC MN

The text of this book is set in Bembo.

Book design by Patrice Sheridan

Manufactured in the United States of America

June 1995

10 9 8 7 6 5 4 3 2 1

For Bob and Patty

C. C. AND J. M.

The violin maker begins with wood. Wood from trees that once grew high in the mountains of Europe. Wood that now stands in the violin maker's house. He will use it to make a violin, a viola, or a cello.

Once the wood has aged for ten years or longer, the violin maker can begin to use it. Sitting quietly in his room, he pets his dog. He listens to beautiful music. He thinks about what he will make. A cello, he decides.

The violin maker looks through his stacks of wood, choosing the pieces he wants. For the top plate, he needs spruce that is light but strong, with a fine, even grain. For the back plate and the sides and neck, he needs curly maple. That wood has a pattern like dancing flames and a straight, even grain to carry true tones and quick vibrations.

To begin each plate, he planes and squares the wide edges of two large, wedge-shaped pieces. When they fit just right, he glues the two pieces together. After they are glued, he attaches large clamps to help hold them in place.

While the glue dries, he walks in the park with his dog. The violin maker remembers when he was a boy. Then he made airplanes that soared like birds. He hurries home, eager to look at the glue joints, eager to work on the cello.

The glue is dry and the pieces are joined tightly. He removes the clamps. He planes the insides of the plates flat. With a pencil, he traces a cello outline. Putting on his ear protectors, he starts the band saw. *E-e-e-e!* He cuts out the rough cello shape.

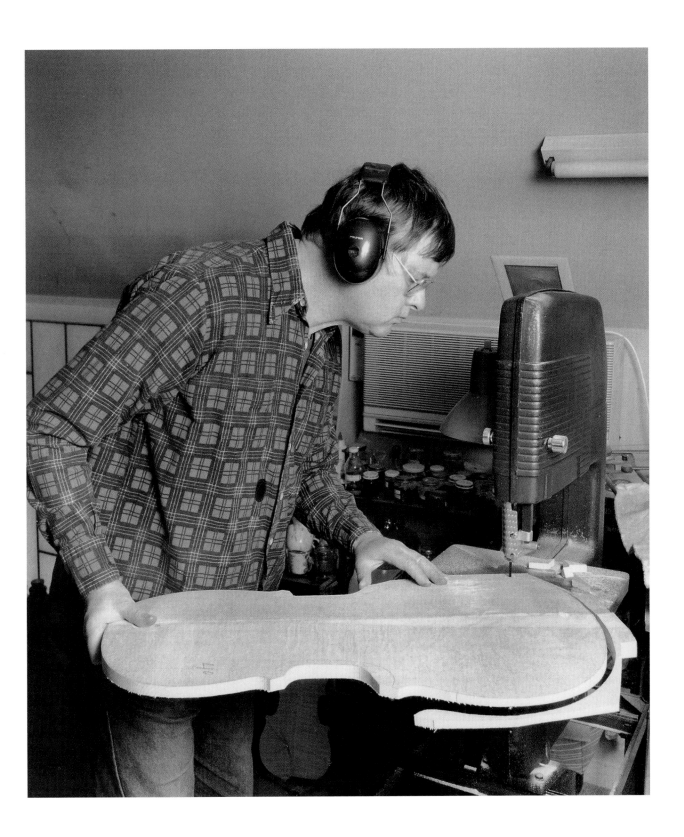

A hard part comes next. The outside of the top and back must be shaped. No machines are used. The violin maker's muscles push gouges and large planes. After many strokes, wide, curled shavings cover the workbench and spill onto the floor and the violin maker's dog.

Knowing that the quality of the sound is influenced by form, the violin maker studies the curved shape as he carves. He sees when the arching is right. It is time to use smaller planes. *Scra-ape! Scra-a-ape!* Thousands of small, curled shavings fly off the planes onto the workbench, the floor, and the sleeping dog.

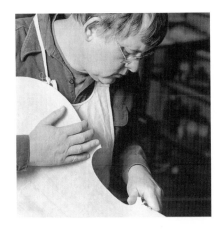

With the arching nearly completed, the violin maker finishes the edges, then marks and cuts a shallow, narrow groove near them. Into this groove he inlays curved pieces of decorative purfling. At each corner, he narrows the purfling to a fine, graceful point.

He finishes the arching to perfection with scrapers, sharp files, and fine sand-paper. Just a little sanding. Too much can spoil the precision of the arching.

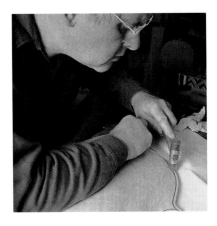

One side is still flat. Time for more hard work. Gouges and planes bite out the insides of the plates. Pieces fly! Shavings fall. Again and again the violin maker stops to measure the thicknesses of the plates. They must have the exact stiffness he wants. Plates that are too thick or too thin will produce weak or dull tones.

When he has removed almost enough wood, he is ready to use his small planes and scrapers. *Scra-a-tch! Scra-a-ape!* Brush the dust away. *Poof!* Blow the dust away. With his calipers, he measures one last time. The plates are nearly finished.

All that remain to be made are the sound holes and a bass bar. The sound holes, shaped like the letter *f*, must be cut into the top. The flowing tones of the cello will come through the *f* holes. The violin maker must position the holes exactly. He measures carefully before he traces on the *f* pattern. He drills a little hole at the edge of the *f* tracing. The blade of a coping saw is removable. It goes through the hole. Slowly, carefully, the violin maker saws along the line he drew until he has cut all the way around. Out falls the *f*. With knives he smooths the edges of the holes.

Lightly holding a plate, the violin maker taps it to listen for pitch. When the plates are perfectly tuned, no more wood needs to be removed. Next the violin maker cuts a bass bar from spruce. He fits and glues the long piece of wood inside the top plate. The bar supports the plate and helps it vibrate evenly when the cello is played. Then he carves the bar until it has a beautiful flowing arch, small at the ends, high in the middle. With the bass bar shaped, the plates are done!

Standing them side by side, he stares at their smoothness, their silky whiteness. The violin maker sighs. He feels good. He picks up his fiddle, the last instrument he made. He practices his favorite quartet music. Three friends are coming for an evening of music making. Until today, the violin maker has been too busy to make music.

The cello will make music one day too. It's time to get back to work. He puts his violin into its case. He glances at the finished cello plates and smiles. Now he begins the sides by planing the ribs evenly. Onto a wooden partial-cello form, he glues thick blocks as supports for the cello's thin ribs. He dips the ribs in water and bends them, using a hot iron. *Phew!* Steam rises from the damp wood.

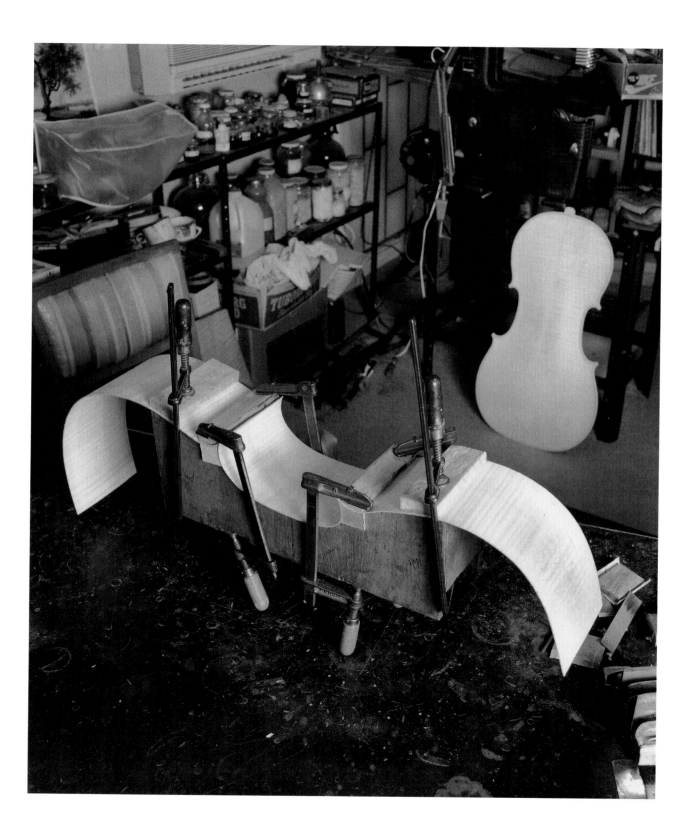

Glued together, the ribs and blocks form the shape of a cello. Along the inside edges of the ribs, the violin maker attaches linings that will help hold the plates in place. When they are dry, he carves the blocks until they are smooth and rounded. Carving, fitting, gluing, waiting. Days pass before he glues the back onto the ribs, holding them together with clamps.

A day later he writes his name, his town, and the year on a small label, which he glues inside. Now he glues on the top. Clamps hold it in place.

The cello is sealed, closed like a box. The luthier's label can be seen through an *f* hole. The elegant bass bar, so carefully carved, is hidden away.

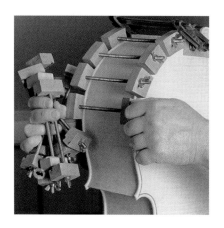

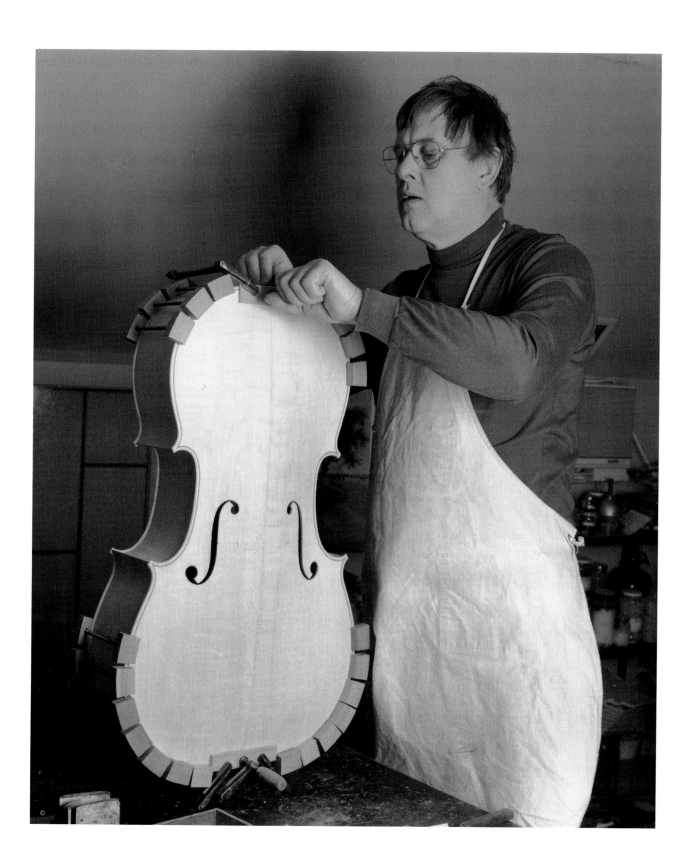

The neck, including the pegbox and graceful scroll, must be made. The violin maker traces an outline onto a solid block of curly maple. Again he uses the squealing band saw to cut away the larger pieces of wood. After he pencils on the scroll design, he forms the graceful curves by hand with gouges, chisels, knives, and files.

Four small holes are drilled through the pegbox before it is hollowed out. Then the violin maker chips out wood, pounding hard with a wooden mallet against a chisel. *Bang! Thump!*

He finishes the scroll with a fluted design, gouging, scraping, and filing the spirals and grooves until they are perfectly curved and smooth. Fine dust covers the dog, but he doesn't look up. He doesn't know that the cello will soon be done. Finishing touches are made to the neck and pegbox. Scraping. *Scra-atch!* Filing. *Shu-ush!* Reaming. *Krr-tch!*

At long last the neck is ready to be fitted into the instrument. The violin maker studies the angle and cuts away a paper-thin slice of wood before deciding that the neck stands just right. Not too high, not too low. He glues and clamps it. He waits a whole day for it to dry before he files and sands it once more.

With a sponge dampened in water, he wipes the cello clean—the neck, the scroll, the plates, the ribs. When the wood is dry, he sands all the surfaces ever so lightly with his finest sandpaper. The cello is finished "in the white."

It is ready for varnish. The violin maker puts away his tools and cleans his workbench and desk. He vacuums the floor. He finds his brushes. He brushes on one, two, three layers of transparent undercoating, a filler that enhances the beauty of the grain and keeps the wood from absorbing the colored varnish.

Swish! He brushes on the first coat of varnish. The room smells of turpentine, exotic resins, and alcohol.

Varnishing takes days and days. Each coat must dry before the next one is applied. Each coat adds luster and more intense color to the cello. After several layers of thin varnish, the violin maker polishes the cello with a soft cloth, oil, and pumice, removing dust and imperfections. More varnish, more color, more polishing. Gradually the cello changes from a light yellow, to deep yellow, to yellow brown.

While the violin maker waits for the varnish to dry, he walks his dog, practices his violin, sharpens his tools, and starts making another instrument, a viola.

After eight to ten more coats of varnish, the cello's color changes to a golden, reddish brown. The varnish is dry. The cello glistens, the flames jump.

It is time to set up the cello. The violin maker glues on the fingerboard. Into the pegbox he fits four pegs. He fits the endbutton and cuts a bridge and a nut. He makes a soundpost. Slipping it inside the cello through an *f* hole, he stands it up between the top and back, adjusting it precisely, because the position of the soundpost influences the tone and resonance of the plates.

Later, when there are no more pieces left to fit, the violin maker puts on the strings, adjusting them over the bridge and tightening them around the pegs. The cello is finished. It's ready to be played.

The violin maker admires his new cello and watches the flames in the wood grain reflect in the light. He can see its outside beauty, but he cannot know its inside beauty, for this violin maker does not play the cello. He has to wait for the cellist. Then he'll finally hear the music in the wood.

GLOSSARY

BAROQUE CELLO   A cello made to play music the way it was written between 1600 and 1750. It is held between the knees to be played. The cello in this book is a baroque cello.

BRIDGE   An elaborately carved piece of lightweight maple that supports the strings above the instrument. The player bows the strings between the bridge and the fingerboard.

ENDBUTTON   A small, rounded piece of wood inserted into the end-block. The cord of the tailpiece is wrapped around it. A modern cello has an enlarged endbutton with a hole through the middle. A metal endpin slides through it, in and out of the cello. The cello stands on the endpin when it is played. The baroque cello has no end-pin.

FINGERBOARD   A long piece of ebony fitted and glued onto the flat part of the neck. Four pegs fit into the pegbox. The strings wrap around the pegs, fall into the grooves of the nut, and pass over the fingerboard and across the bridge.

NECK, PEGBOX, AND SCROLL   A single piece of wood carved and attached to the body of the instrument. The scroll is decorative. The pegbox holds the pegs.

NUT   A small piece of ebony glued onto the neck at the end of the fingerboard. It has four grooves with the proper spacing for the strings. It is slightly higher than the fingerboard.

PLATES   The carved top and back of an instrument. The top is also called the belly or the table.

PURFLING   A strip of light-colored wood glued between two strips of black wood to form one strip, like a sandwich. Six of these strips fit into a groove near the edge of each plate to form a continuous line for decoration. Purfling also protects the edges of the plates.

RIBS   The sides of the instrument. The wood is planed thin and bent into the same shape as the plates. When the plates are glued onto the ribs, the body of the instrument is complete.

SOUNDPOST   A wooden cylinder about eleven millimeters thick. The ends are cut to fit the arching of the plates. The soundpost stands firmly between the two plates.

TAILPIECE   A carved, triangular piece of wood made to keep the strings taut. It is held by the strings and an endbutton.

VIOLIN MAKER   A person who crafts stringed instruments such as the violin, viola, violoncello (cello), and double bass. Also called a luthier.

Roel Dieltiens plays his new cello.